Immortals

HERO

Dragon

Steve Barlow and Steve Skidmore

Illustrated by Jack Lawrence

Franklin Watts
First published in Great Britain in 2015 by The Watts Publishing Group

PB ISBN 978 1 4451 4081 0
ebook ISBN 978 1 4451 4082 7
Library ebook ISBN 978 1 4451 4083 4

1 3 5 7 9 10 8 6 4 2

Printed and bound by CPI Group (UK) Ltd, Croydon, CR0 4YY

FSC
www.fsc.org
MIX
Paper from
responsible sources
FSC® C104740

Franklin Watts
An imprint of
Hachette Children's Group
Part of The Watts Publishing Group
Carmelite House
50 Victoria Embankment
London EC4Y 0DZ

An Hachette UK Company
www.hachette.co.uk

www.franklinwatts.co.uk

How to be a hero

This book is not like others you have read. This is a choose-your-own-destiny book where YOU are the hero of this adventure.

Each section of this book is numbered. At the end of most sections, you will have to make a choice. Each choice will take you to a different section of the book.

If you choose correctly, you will succeed. But be careful. If you make a bad choice, you may have to start the adventure again. If this happens, make sure you learn from your mistake!

Go to the next page to start your adventure. And remember, don't be a zero, be a hero!

Long ago, in the Old Kingdom, lived a race of people called Dragon Warriors. They could use an ancient spell to transform themselves into dragons. With fiery breath and armoured scales that no weapon could pierce, the dragons helped to keep peace across the world.

Over the years, fewer Dragon Warriors were born, until only one remained. You are the last of the Dragon Warriors. You live in the city of Drake's Rest. You are taught Dragon-lore by Morlana, the Keeper of the Sacred Grove.

It is a bright midwinter morning when you receive a message from Morlana, summoning you to the Sacred Grove.

Now go to 1.

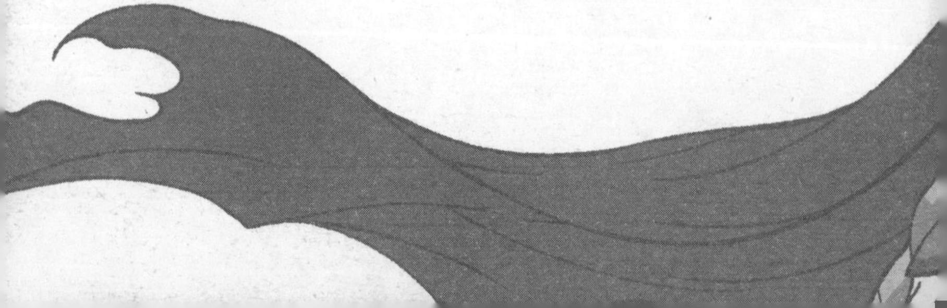

1

Morlana is waiting for you in the Sacred Grove. A dwarf stands by her side.

You bow. "My lady Morlana, you summoned me."

She nods. "We need you, Dragon Warrior. This is Brylin. He has travelled a great distance with news of disturbing events in the Outlands. Speak, Brylin."

The dwarf begins his story. "An ancient power has emerged from deep within the Iron Mines. An army of barbarians has poured out from beneath the earth, bringing death and destruction to villages and towns. The army is led by Grull the Cruel. He is marching here, vowing to destroy the people of the Old Kingdom."

"Then Grull must be stopped," you say.

To transform into dragon form straight away, go to 15.

To find out more about Grull, go to 36.

2

You chant the Dragon Warrior spell and change back into dragon form.

You take out the manticores with a fireball, before they can react. The enemy is consumed by the flames!

But your plan to sneak into the camp is finished – you will have to attack!

Go to 19.

3

You say the Dragon Warrior spell and turn into a dragon. With a great flap of your wings you soar into the sky, heading for the Iron Mines.

Some time later as you fly over the long valley of the Old Kingdom, you see a plume of black smoke rising up into the sky.

To investigate the smoke, go to 43.
If you wish to fly on, go to 23.

4

You fly towards the fearsome creatures but they create an icestorm, blinding you.

Before you can react, the giants grab hold of you with their monstrous hands. They begin to tear at your wings.

To try and break free, go to 44.
To blast the giants with fire, go to 37.

5

You look around for cover and see a small cave in a rocky cliff. You run towards it and head inside.

Minutes later, the goblins pass by on their wolves.

You wait until you think they have gone and make your way out of the cave.

You feel a heavy blow to the head and crash to the floor. The goblins were waiting for you!

"I told you I could smell something bad!" laughs one of the goblins.

"Let's eat it!" suggests another.

"No, let's take it to Grull!"

To transform into a dragon and fly away, go to 42.

To change into a dragon and attack the goblins, go to 49.

To let the goblins take you to Grull, go to 21.

6

"Tell me where I will find Grull," you say.

Brylin splutters as he laughs. "He is in the Eastern Swamp, but he is heading here. He will find you and destroy you."

Before you can continue to question Brylin, he launches himself at you. He knocks you to the ground with a crunching blow. Suddenly, a flash of light sends Brylin flying backwards. Morlana has stopped Grull's servant in his tracks.

Go to 20.

7

"I know how to defeat Morlana and her Dragon Warrior," you reply.

"And why would you want to tell me this?" asks Grull.

You hold up the Dragon Ring. "I want power. I have managed to steal this ring from the Sacred Grove, but I need someone to help me use it..."

Grull's eyes glint. "Bring me the ring."

He orders his guards to let you approach.

You move forward carefully. You are now within striking distance.

If you wish to attack the roc, go to 35.

If you wish to attack Grull, go to 22.

8

You speed towards your enemies. You send a jet of flame through the air and they suddenly split up. You crash into a taurogriff with your claws out, tearing the rider from his saddle. You go to spin away but the other two taurogriffs smash into you. You feel your wing tear as one of the creatures catches you with its deadly horn.

To continue the fight, go to 25.

To break off the fight, go to 38.

9

You are exhausted so you decide to land. You transform back into human form and eat some of your provisions before resting.

Go to 26.

10

You chant the transformation spell. As you change into dragon form you breathe out smoke into the air. Brylin cannot see!

A sweep of your tail sends Brylin sprawling across the grove. His axe spins from his grasp and sticks in the soil. The dwarf crashes into a tree and falls to the ground, stunned. As you walk over to him you change back into human form.

To attack Brylin again, go to 31.
If you wish to question him, go to 6.

11

You send a fireball at one of the giants, hitting it in the chest.

But the second giant leaps at you and lands on your back. You try to shake it off, but the creature squeezes your throat, stopping your ability to create fire. He forces you to land on an icy ledge. The other giant grabs hold of you.

Go to 44.

12

You don't want to hit the villagers, so you dive at the goblins, open your jaws and grab at them with your claws. Suddenly a bolt of lightning crackles through the air, narrowly missing you. It came from the ground! The goblins have a spellcaster! You scan the ground and easily spot the spellcaster wearing a bright floppy hat. Before she can cast another spell you swing round and plunge downwards, crushing her under your claws.

A blast of flame sends the remaining goblins running for their lives.

Some of the surviving villagers emerge and are amazed as you return to human form. You explain who you are and tell them about your quest.

"We may be able to help you," says the village leader. "These goblins spoke of seeing Grull in the Eastern Swamp."

You thank the villagers and decide to head for the swamp.

Go to 45.

13

You move towards Grull and try to blow a sheet of fire at him, but you are too weak.

Grull laughs and sprints from the tent. He has escaped! Pain spreads through your body. There is only one thing you can do.

Go to 34.

14

You fly along the mountain range. After many hours you have still not reached a way around. You realise that time is running out.

To head over the mountains, go to 32.

To continue flying around the mountains, go to 26.

15

"I will take dragon form and find Grull," you tell Morlana. But Morlana holds up a hand. "Patience, Dragon Warrior. First we need to know more about our enemy."

You realise that she is right.

Go to 36.

16

You send a fire bolt at the ice bridge. The bridge melts and suddenly breaks apart, sending the ice giants plunging down onto the hard rocks far below.

After another hour of flying you pass over the tops of the mountains and glide down towards the Eastern Swamp. You are exhausted from your efforts, and know that the coming battle will be hard.

If you wish to fly on to find Grull and his army, go to 28.

If you wish to land and rest, go to 9.

17

You raise your claws and fly at the ice giants. But you have little strength to fight these creatures. They swat you away and throw more huge blocks of ice at you.

To use fire against the giants, go to 24.

To continue to attack them with your claws, go to 4.

18

You decide to fly on, but at that moment the air is lit up by a bolt of lightning that comes from the ground!

The bolt stuns you, and you begin to drop from the sky.

Go to 34.

19

You fly at speed towards the camp. Suddenly the night sky is lit up by hundreds of flares – the enemy know that you are here!

You spit dozens of exploding fireballs into the middle of the camp, taking out hundred's of Grull's troops.

As you continue your attack, the air is filled with a great shrieking noise. You look to your left and see a monstrous bird heading towards you. It is a roc. Even you will not be able to defeat such an enemy! It smashes into you, ripping open your flesh with its deadly talons.

Go to 34.

20

"You must find Grull and destroy him," says Morlana as the smoke clears.

She hands you a golden ring. "This is the Ring of Dragons," she tells you. "If you find yourself in peril and cannot escape, say the words 'fly me home'. The ring's magic will bring you back to this time and place, where you can begin your quest again. It also has the power to heal any injury you have received if you transform. Use it wisely."

You place the ring on your finger. Now you must decide where you will head.

If you wish to head to the Eastern Swamp, go to 45.

If you wish to head towards the Iron Mines, go to 3.

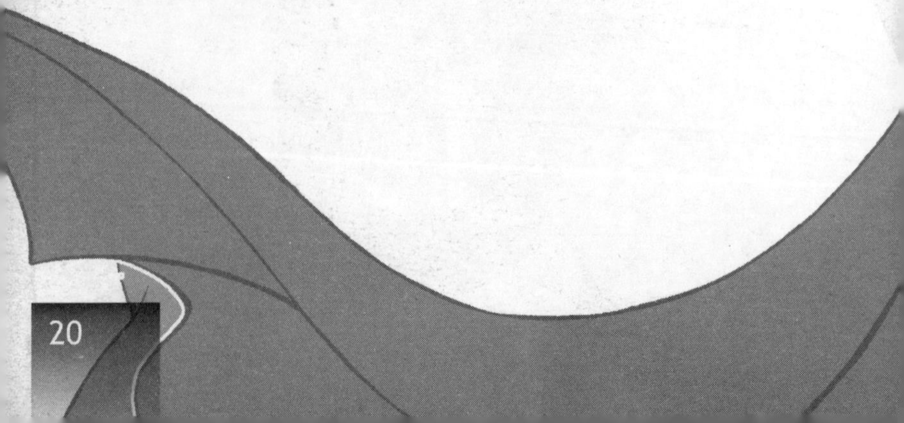

21

"Take it to Grull?" sneers one of the goblins. "No, I'm hungry! It's dinner time!"

He grabs you and licks his lips. It looks as though you're the main course!

Go to 34.

22

You chant the spell and transform into dragon form.

But before you can attack Grull, the roc speeds towards you and takes hold of your neck in its monstrous talons. You cannot breathe!

"So, you are really the Dragon Warrior," snarls Grull. "I thought this must be a trick! Kill him my beauty!" he orders. The roc's talons begin to crush your neck.

Go to 34.

23

As you fly on, the air is filled with arrows.

You spin around. Looking down you see a village being attacked by a band of goblins. They have set fire to some huts and have now turned their attention to you.

More arrows head your way. They don't really bother you, as you know they can't pierce your dragon scales. But then a lightning bolt flashes up from the ground, stunning you. The goblins have a spellcaster! You begin to fall from the sky and you realise there is only one thing you can do.

Go to 34.

24

You send a great stream of fire at the blocks of ice, melting them before they can hit you.

The giants roar, sending a snowstorm your way. Again your fiery breath vaporises it.

If you wish to attack your enemies with your claws, go to 4.

To blast the giants with fire, go to 37.

25

Ignoring your injured wing, you bank left and spit out a fireball at the nearest taurogriff. It bursts into flames and drops away.

The other barbarian breaks off the attack. He turns his taurogriff around and speeds away.

If you decide to let your enemy escape, go to 33.

If you want to give chase and destroy him, go to 47.

26

Many hours later you see a great owl heading towards you.

You recognise it as being one of Morlana's messengers. It lands on your shoulder and speaks. "Dragon Warrior, you have taken too long. Grull has arrived at Drake's Rest. You have failed to protect us. You must begin your quest again."

Go to 34.

27

"It seems strange that you know so much about Grull. Perhaps he sent you here?"

There is a moment's pause as the dwarf realises you know his secret. He reaches for his axe. "My master, Grull, commands me to kill the Dragon Warrior!"

He swings his weapon at you, but you manage to avoid it. Again he attacks.

To turn into a dragon, go to 10.

To ask Morlana for help, go to 40.

28

You are tired but you know that time is running out to find Grull. You fly on towards the swamp.

Darkness has already fallen when you pass into a desolate valley. Ahead of you are thousands of campfires, lighting up the marshes. You have found Grull's army!

If you wish to attack immediately, go to 19.

If you wish to land and make a plan, go to 41.

29

You bank sideways and speed through the sky.

The taurogriffs give chase. They are faster than you and close in.

You spin and dive in an attempt to shake off your pursuers, but they follow your every move.

To attack your enemy, go to 8.

If you wish to try and escape, go to 38.

30

You transform back into human form and head towards the camp.

It takes some time for you to make your way through the wet marshland.

Nearing the camp you see a patrol of grey ghost knights mounted on giant scorpion-like manticores. They see you, speed towards you and order you to surrender.

If you wish to try and escape, go to 2.

To obey the knights, go to 46.

31

You grab Brylin and he struggles. Finally, he breaks free from you, but stumbles over a tree root. He lands on his sharp axe blade.

Morlana shakes her head. "You should have questioned him. We might have found out more about Grull's plans and where he is."

"It is too late for that," you say.

Go to 20.

32

You head higher into the sky over the mountains. The air is thin and it takes all of your strength to continue flying.

Suddenly you see a huge block of ice heading through the air towards you. You spin away, narrowly avoiding it. Ahead of you are two ice giants throwing more blocks of ice at you!

To attack them with fire, go to 24.

To attack them with your claws, go to 17.

33

You realise that your injured wing will stop you from catching the taurogriff.

You glide down and land, where you change back into human form.

At that moment you hear a baying noise.

In the distance you see a pack of gigantic three-headed wolves being ridden by goblins.

If you wish to try and find somewhere to hide, go to 5.

To change back into a dragon and fly away, go to 42.

To change back into a dragon and attack the goblins, go to 49.

34

You call on the power of the Dragon Ring. "Fly me home!" you cry.

There is a roar of flame as you pass through time and space.

You find yourself back in the Sacred Grove. Morlana is seated on the dragon seat. She shakes her head. "You must be more careful in your choices. Begin your quest again!"

If you wish to head to the Eastern Swamp, go to 45.

If you wish to head towards the Iron Mines, go to 3.

35

You transform into dragon form and breathe a stream of flame at the roc. It is engulfed by fire.

It tries to fly away, but only manages to hit the tent walls, which catch alight. There is total confusion as Grull's guards try to escape the inferno. The roc staggers around, setting alight anything in its path, before finally crashing to the floor, dead.

Grull leaps from his throne, snatches a lance from one of the guards and hurls it at you. It pierces your chest! The tip is made from taurogriff horn! You stagger backwards in shock and pain.

"You are finished, Dragon Warrior!" screams Grull. "I have beaten you!"

If you wish to return to the grove, go to 34.

If you wish to destroy Grull, go to 13.

If you wish to try and take him prisoner, go to 39.

36

"Tell me more about Grull's army," you say to Brylin.

"It is a mighty force," he replies. "It sweeps through the land destroying towns and villages. No one can stand up to its power. Those who refuse to join it are killed."

You stare at the dwarf. Then how did you escape? you wonder.

To question Brylin, go to 27.

To let him continue with his story, go to 48.

37

You shoot a fireball at the giants, causing them to stagger backwards. Another blast forces the creatures to retreat onto a bridge of ice.

To attack the giants with more fireballs, go to 11.

To use your claws to attack the giants, go to 44.

To blast the bridge of ice, go to 16.

38

You cannot shake off your attackers. The taurogriffs move in for the kill.

You swish at one of the creatures with your tail and send it spinning through the sky. Another taurogriff slams into you with its deadly horns and there is nothing you can do.

Go to 34.

39

You are the Dragon Warrior, the last of your race! If Grull escapes he will destroy everyone in the Old Kingdom! You ignore the pain and grasp the lance. You pull it from your chest. Grull looks on in horror as you snatch him up in your claws.

With the last of your strength you beat your wings and fly out of the tent, carrying Grull screaming into the night.

Below you his army is fleeing. Without a leader they are no longer a threat.

You head for home...

Go to 50.

40

"Mistress, help me," you cry.

As Brylin's axe cuts through the air, Morlana holds out her hand. A wave of energy engulfs the dwarf and throws him across the grove and into a tree. His axe spins from his hands.

If you wish to fight Brylin, go to 31.
If you wish to question him, go to 6.

41

You land away from the camp and decide what to do. The army is large, so if you are going to attack, then you will have to do it quickly and try to surprise them.

You also think that by changing back into human form you could sneak into the camp.

To attack the camp in dragon form, go to 19.

To transform into human form, go to 30.

42

You transform into dragon form.

With a flick of your wings you head into the sky. Even with your injured wing you are soon far away from the goblins. After some time you see a huge mountain range reaching high into the sky. These mountains are the home of the ice giants. You have to decide whether to fly over the mountains, or take the longer but safer route around them.

To fly over the mountains, go to 32.

To fly around the mountains, go to 14.

43

You fly towards the smoke and see dozens of goblins attacking a village. They are shooting burning arrows at the huts, setting them alight.

Captured villagers are being rounded up and threatened by the ugly creatures.

To help the villagers, go to 12.

If you think this is none of your business, go to 18.

44

You swipe at the ice giants with your claws, but your efforts are useless.

The giants' icicle-sharp teeth tear your wings before they throw you over the side of the mountain. You plunge helplessly through the cold air.

Go to 34.

45

You say the transformation spell and turn into dragon form. A mighty flap of your wings sends you soaring high into the eastern sky.

Some time later you see a flight of eagles heading towards you. You peer into the darkening sky and realise that they are not ordinary eagles. They are taurogriffs, armed with huge, razor-sharp horns which could even damage a dragon! They are ridden by Grull's clansmen.

To try to out fly the creatures, go to 29.
To attack the creatures, go to 8.

46

You hold up your hands. "I must speak to Grull," you say. "I have important information about Drake's Rest. I know its weak points, but I will only reveal them to Grull."

The ghost knights hold a brief conversation before deciding to grant you your request.

You are on your way to Grull! But your smile is short lived as you are stung by a manticore's tail. You pass out.

Some time later you awake to find yourself in a huge tent. There are dozens of guards of all races and forms.

Grull sits on a throne. Standing behind him is a monstrous bird. It is a roc – the most fearsome bird in the world!

"So, human. What information do you have about Drake's Rest?" asks Grull.

If you want to talk to Grull, go to 7.

If you wish to change into dragon form immediately, go to 22.

47

You speed after the taurogriff, but your injured wing is unable to take the strain. It begins to rip apart and you drop towards the ground. Glancing back, your enemy realises that you are injured and turns back to attack.

You spit a stream of fire at the taurogriff, but it avoids your attack and heads in for the kill. With such an injury to your wing, you realise that you cannot defend yourself.

Go to 34.

48

"Continue your story," you say.

Instead of replying, Brylin reaches for his axe. "My master, Grull, will destroy you all!" he cries. "I must kill the last Dragon Warrior!"

He swings his weapon at you, but as you jump out of the way, you lose your balance and stagger to the ground. The dwarf stands above you, axe raised.

To fight Brylin, go to 31.
To ask Morlana for help, go to 40.

49

You transform with a roar and fly full speed at the goblins. Their arrows bounce off your scales. You blast them with a stream of fire.

You fly on. In the distance you see some huge mountains, reaching high into the sky. They are the home of the ice giants. It will be faster to fly over the mountains, but the route around them will be safer.

To fly over the mountains, go to 32.
To fly around the mountains, go to 14.

50

You arrive back at the Sacred Grove and deliver Grull to Morlana.

"He will be tried and held to account for his crimes," she says. She beckons her guards to take him away.

You change back into human form and hand back the Dragon Ring. Morlana smiles. "Well done, Dragon Warrior. I knew we could rely on you. You are a true hero!"

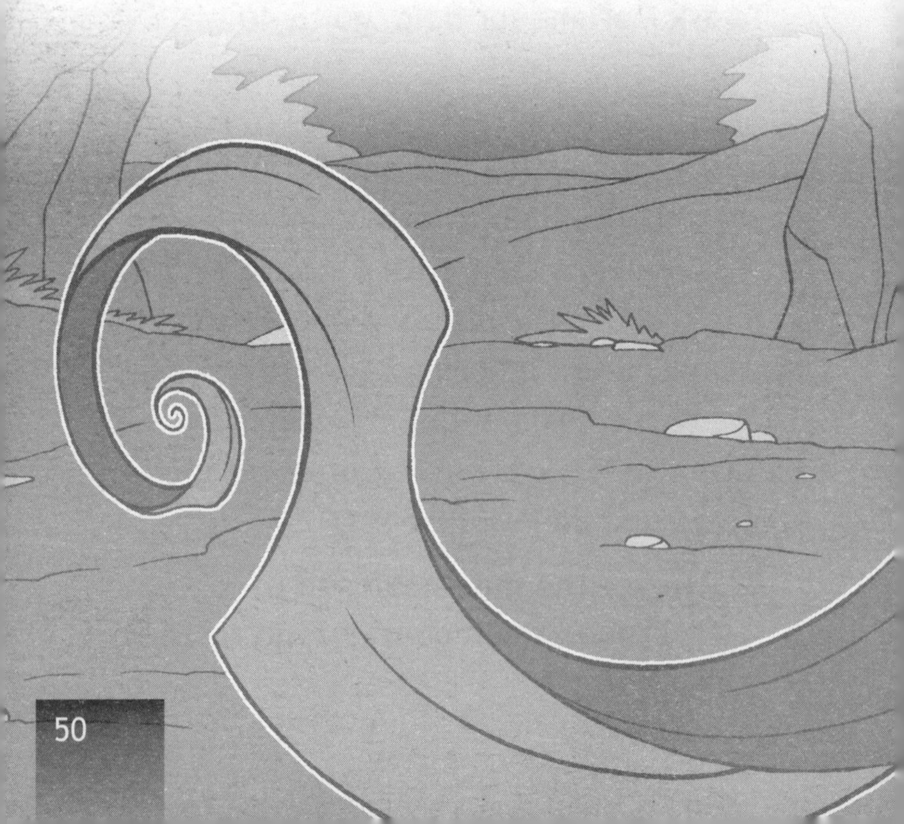

I HERO Quiz

Test yourself with this special quiz. It has been designed to see how much you remember about the book you've just read. Can you get all five answers right?

Download answer sheets from:

https://www.hachettechildrens.co.uk/Teacher%27s%20Zone/non_fiction_activity_sheets.page

Question 1

Where do you meet Morlana at the start of the adventure?

A Eastern Swamp

B Sacred Grove

C Drake's Rest

D Iron Mines

Question 2

Where do you eventually find Grull's army?

A Drake's Rest

B Eastern Swamp

C the mountains

D Sacred Grove

Question 3

What type of bird does Grull have?

A a roc

B a parrot

C an owl

D a taurogriff

Question 4

What was Brylin's mission?

A capture Morlana

B kill the Dragon Warrior

C steal the Ring of Dragons

D destroy the Sacred Grove

Question 5

What did Grull want to do?

A find the Ring of Dragons

B destroy the Sacred Grove

C destroy the people of the Old Kingdom

D be a Dragon Warrior

About the 2Steves

"The 2Steves" are Britain's most popular writing double act for young people, specialising in comedy and adventure. They perform regularly in schools and libraries, and at festivals, taking the power of words and story to audiences of all ages.

Together they have written many books, including the *Crime Team* series. Find out what they've been up to at: **www.the2steves.net**

About the illustrator: Jack Lawrence

Jack Lawrence is a successful freelance comics illustrator, working on titles such as *A.T.O.M.*, Cartoon Network, *Doctor Who Adventures*, *2000 AD*, *Gogos Mega Metropolis* and *Spider-Man Tower of Power*. He also works as a freelance toy designer.

Jack lives in Maidstone in Kent with his partner and two cats.